Whispers of Spring

Linda Boulanger

Whispers of Spring
A Wings & Whispers Love Story
©2021 by Linda Boulanger

Released first in Kaleidoscope Hearts Vol. 3 Anthology
Edited by Grace Augustine/Edits with a Touch of Grace
Cover Design/Interior Design by Tell~Tale Book Covers

Published by TreasureLine Publishing
ISBN: 978-1-61752-220-8

PRINTED IN THE UNITED STATES OF AMERICA

I dedicate this book to
everyone who has ever needed someone to help them
and to those who've been willing to risk all to do so.

Join me *Between the Pages* for news and special offers…

You'll receive news about my writing, information on sales
and promos, and also a couple of free books for signing up.
You'll find the sign-up form and information at this link:

LindaBoulangerBooks.com/newsletter-sign-up

Chapter 1

The slightest hint of sunshine peeked through the clouds just before the skies opened and began to dump more snow onto the already covered ground. For a split second, Adam felt a ray of excitement only to have it doused by a million tiny, frozen crystals. It may have been beautiful, but he was tired of the snow. That had been one of the best things about being sent to an island full of dragon shifters, fairies, and other angels, even if his going there hadn't made sense. What magical being needed a guardian angel?

Apparently, none considering he hadn't been presented with his next case. Adam felt a sense of defeat when the thought about the fact that he'd been without a charge for months and months, even before he'd been sent to Hernathea. He'd thought he'd find his next assignment waiting for him once he reached the island. Now, he was thinking perhaps coming here was some sort of punishment for voicing his discontent at being passed over for one mission after another. He couldn't help his irritation. What good was a guardian angel who had no one to watch over?

Worse yet, the job that had been set up for him was that of a solar panel installer. He looked at the snow and the clouds, both of which had been hanging around ever since he'd arrived, doing their best to obscure what little light was needed to effectively use the solar panels.

He groaned and scrubbed a hand across the dark crop

of short, immaculately styled hair atop his head. There was a real disconnect somewhere. It was as if the Logic Department at the Guardians' Headquarters had pulled ideas out of a bag, paired them up, and went out to lunch to never return.

None of that actually existed. In reality, Adam had no idea who called the shots, other than the Big Guy. But who made it happen, and how, were beyond him. He'd simply wake up to find a big manilla envelope with his name on it laying in an obvious spot in whatever place he was calling home at the time. Inside would be all the information and funding he'd need for his next mission. The last envelope he'd received had been different. It had contained nothing but a plane ticket, a debit card, and the name of a gentleman who would be meeting him at the airport.

The man ended up being his boss, Art Guthrie. He owned The Solar System—a company that installed and maintained solar panels for energy purposes, although they had expanded into solar powered Christmas decorations and other yard adornments over the holidays. Fortunately, they took a lot less sunlight to operate than the huge panels. Hiring Adam out to put them up and again to take them down was what had been keeping the business afloat during this peculiarly snowy period.

At least that's what Art said. Hernathea, it seemed, was one of those places where people came to warm up during the time when the rest of the world was blanketed in white. Except for a few days around Christmas, when some sort of magic provision allowed for snow wishes, the weather stayed pretty even. Fall and Spring were a little cooler than the comfortable but warm summer, and the temps of winter dropped just a tad lower… none of it included weeks of wet, white powder.

Except this year. They were at the point where more than a few people were wondering if something had gone wrong. As far as Adam was concerned, it sure had. He didn't really mind the cold, or even the snow. Most of the time. He huffed. All things considered, if he wasn't going to have a charge, at least *they* could have given him some good vacation weather.

As if to remind him he wasn't on vacation, the snow intensified. Adam grumbled and grasped the steering wheel a bit tighter as the big work truck fishtailed. A quick glance at the dashboard showed the temps had dropped even farther in the last few minutes.

Adam looked up just in time to see something big and white dashing right into his path. H screamed and slammed on the brakes, instantly realizing that was a bad move. The truck slid sideways, first one way and then the other as he spun the steering wheel in an attempt to straighten out, all while trying to figure out where the big white blob had ended up.

Just as he regained control of the truck, *it* appeared again, right before him, leaving him no choice but to point the front end of the vehicle toward what he hoped was the side of the road to keep from hitting it.

A jostle, a jump, and a bump later, the truck came to a stop and Adam realized the side of the road was actually a ditch filled with snow. And now, his truck was buried in fluff halfway up the door. Great, he thought as he began trying to force the door against the snow, beating out a space just large enough for him to get out.

Jumping out, the snow instantly caked to him as he pushed against it while making his way to the road. He clawed his way up to the packed surface, glad he'd grabbed the gloves he'd worn when packing up Mr. Vincent's old solar panels. They weren't old, really. Just not as new as his new ones.

It was a long story, but the man had decided he needed bigger panels because he wasn't producing enough power to sell back to the municipal power plant of Hernathea. The truth was his panels were fine. The non-existent sunlight was the problem. The panels were making and storing enough to run his big house, just not a lot of excess.

Adam shrugged knowing his boss had tried to reason with the gentleman. In the end, they'd made him a special deal on larger panels and their installment. Art Guthrie was a firm believer in the old adage that the customer was always right.

Standing up and attempting without success to brush himself off, Adam looked back at the half-buried truck. Mr. Guthrie may change his tune when he learned it had resulted in his truck being banked in a snowdrift. Probably not, Adam thought as he turned to survey the area. The too swift motion had him sliding, his arms windmilling in his effort to stay upright. Gravity won and he landed in a heap, his eyes widening as he saw the white blob galloping toward him as he went down.

It took him a few seconds for it to finally sink in that

the mystery blob was actually a huge, furry, white dog. He'd never seen a dog so big… or slobbery! Adam's face was covered in wet kisses as the dog stood over him, its excited tail wagging its whole body.

"Whoa, buddy! Slow down." He laughed and pushed the mass away just enough so he could roll away and to his feet. He found it odd that the glass-like ice that had caused him to fall moments ago had given way to compressed snow that he was, at least, able to stand on.

"I'm not complaining," he whispered, looking skyward. If anything, he was thankful, especially considering he was out in the middle of nowhere with poor cell service and a crazy dog companion who looked like he might come in for another tackle at any moment. At least the snow had let up some, giving him the opportunity to look around.

"Now what?" he asked the dog. "Do you think we can walk all the way back to town?"

The dog barked, turned a couple of tight circles, jumped toward him and then took off toward the other side of the road. He ran a few steps before looking back to bark at Adam. Two more whirls and he was off again.

Adam's brows lifted, then fell as he squinted at the dog, wondering how he was managing to keep from sinking. He knew the beast weighed at least as much as he did, if not more, and the place he was standing should have put him over his head in snow, not up to his doggie kneecaps… or whatever they were called. There had to be a road there.

"Hey!" he called. "Is this the way to your house?"

White Blob didn't answer, he just kept going, looking over his shoulder to bark every few steps.

"All right. I'll follow," Adam called to him.

At that point, he felt he had little to lose. Hopefully, if it were a wild goose chase, he would be able to find his way back to the main road. On the other hand, maybe there was a warm house with a telephone he could use to call for help, or even a truck that could pull him out.

Crossing gloved fingers, he picked his way along the path created by the dog prints, happy to see a mailbox just before they changed directions. This route was more obviously a road. The thick canopy of trees above having kept the snow to a minimum allowed bits of gravel and grass to peek through the carpet of white in a few places. He might be mistaken, because his nose was so cold, but he thought he smelled the scent of smoke from a fireplace.

"Good job," he told the dog who had begun to walk right beside him except when he'd dart after a scampering squirrel.

Up ahead, the trees cleared and Adam's smile stung his cold cheeks when he saw a dwelling take shape. It looked more like a barn, but he was fairly sure there was a house beyond that. He squinted and was able to make out a lovely old two-story farmhouse. He tried to quicken his pace, but the snow was deeper the closer they got to the buildings. The lack of tire tracks and dark windows had him concerned, though smoke curled out from the top of the chimney. Someone was there.

Adam felt the ground change and realized he must have hit a sidewalk… a sidewalk that was covered with ice beneath the layers of snow. He walked gently, putting one foot in front of the other and making sure he was steady before taking the next step. It made for a slow trek to the porch of the old house, but at least he stayed upright.

His new companion was a constant beside him until he reached the wooden railing and was able to pull himself up the uneven rock steps, though the wood planks at the top were slick as well where the snow had drifted across them, melted, and refrozen. At least that only lasted a couple of feet before he hit dry wood, otherwise he would have slid all the way to the door. He looked around to see White Blob standing at the bottom of the steps, his tail wagging.

"Whew!" Adam told him with a wink. He chuckled to himself and shook his head. It was funny how quickly one could befriend a dog. It was too bad people couldn't trust each other in that manner.

Turning back to the door, a jolt of nervousness shot through him. Could he trust the person on the other side? It wasn't like he had a lot of choices. His truck was buried, and he'd already come this far to find help. He needed to suck it up and get on with it.

Adam swallowed hard and pressed a finger to the doorbell, listening for a second. He couldn't hear a thing. He tried again with the same result so, after a few more seconds, he decided to use the old-fashioned knocker that hung in the middle of the heavy wooden door. He clanked it three times, and again there was no response. Sucking in a deep breath that he blew out slowly, Adam tried one last time, moving away from the door almost the same moment the last clank sounded. He turned to the dog still standing at the bottom of the steps.

"Now what?" he asked the blob who only whimpered a bit before his tail, once again, took control of his body. "The owner has to be around here somewhere, right? Maybe we should check the barn..."

At the edge of the porch, Adam hit the slick wood. His body pitched every which way and his arms flailed before he lost his footing and went down hard. His head contacted the porch and every one of the stone steps as he slid into a heap on the snow-covered sidewalk. Groaning, he tried to open his eyes, but the sky above swam in a psychedelic swirl. He wasn't sure, but he thought he heard a loud bang, and, for a split second, he thought maybe he'd been shot. He'd fallen plenty of times in his life and never had anything like this happen. Guardian angels were pretty tough, they could take a lot of bodily punishment without it affecting them, so it stood to reason he'd done more than just fall.

"Are you okay?"

The sweetest voice he'd ever heard had him forcing his eyes open once again to find a woman leaning over him. He took her in between blinks, focusing first on the near black hair that hung down around her face. It looked as though it would be silky smooth to the touch once combed, but at that moment Adam could see strands and clumps sticking out here and there. They didn't detract at all from the high cheeks and slightly upturned nose that they framed. Rosy pink lips turned downward, expressing her concern almost as much as the dark, well-shaped brows pulled tight above sky-blue eyes.

You're an angel, he thought as his eyes closed again. Only an angel had eyes the color of Heaven.

"Are you hurt?"

Her voice was like a gentle caress... or maybe it was the pressure of her hand barely touching his shoulder... Adam tried to nod, the motion causing him to wince.

"Don't... don't move. I... uh..."

He cracked an eye open just a hair when he felt her move away and watched as she combed her fingers through her hair and chewed on her bottom lip. Adam could tell she was struggling with her decision on what she should do. He didn't blame her. If he'd found a strange man lying in the snow at his doorstep... well, if he were a woman and found himself in that scenario, he'd probably be apprehensive as well.

Her dilemma gave him time to study her a bit more. An oversized sweatshirt and pajama pants couldn't disguise the slender figure beneath, especially the way the shirt hung off one shoulder, exposing the thinness of her neck and upper arm.

For a moment, Adam wondered why she was in her pajamas already, though that thought vanished when he began to push himself into a sitting position and the world around them began to spin.

"I'll be okay, just give me a minute..." he told her... or he at least tried to say those words. He wasn't actually certain just what came out. He looked at her and tried to smile as he slipped back to the snowy ground and his world faded to black.

Chapter 2

Evie wrung her hands together before combing her fingers through her hair in a way she had since she was a small child. Her dad had always said it was a nervous tick. Evie wasn't sure about that, though she did seem to do it in situations of uncertainty.

This was certainly one of those situations! She'd managed to stay secluded at her parents' farm for the last few months. No one at all had encroached on her reclusiveness... until now. Now, she found herself with a strange man crumpled at the bottom of the farmhouse steps. If he didn't die, he'd probably sue her. Or at least try. It wasn't like she had much left to give... or lose.

Evie looked around. This farm was the only thing she had and, quite frankly, she doubted she would be able to maintain her existence there for much longer. She couldn't work the fields because she didn't know the difference between a strand of wheat and a common weed. Selling was inevitable. What little money she had would only feed her and keep the propane tanks from running dry for so long. How could she have been so foolish to have taken for granted what life had given her?

Her poor dad. He must have wondered what he'd done wrong to have been saddled with supporting his two grown daughters and his only grandchild. Only he'd never complained, never seemed unhappy to have all of them around. In fact, it was quite the opposite. Caleb McCormick was a family man through and through. Evie's mom would say that when the girls were away he would grow quiet and subdued. It was as if he gained strength from their presence.

Maybe he did. Although neither of her parents were mystical beings, it had to be in their bloodline somewhere, evidenced by her and her sister both being angels. There was evidence that those whose gifts didn't develop could still absorb the energy of those who had powers.

Evie didn't know much about that. She hadn't given it a lot of thought, to be truthful. Her gift had come in the form of being a sculptor who infused her creations with a magic that would bring contentment to both those who gave them as gifts and to the recipient. She'd focused on her craft, at her dad's urging. He'd tell her that her job was to spread happiness while his was to keep a roof over her head and her belly full.

They'd all laughed at that... except no one was laughing now. She'd lost just about everything, including her desire to sculpt, when she'd lost her parents, her sister, and her... niece. Yes, her niece.

So many times, she'd prayed and asked why she'd been spared. She hated living with the heartache that tormented her every single waking moment of every single day.

Yet there she was. Each morning at six a.m. on the dot, just like they always had, her eyes would open. She'd throw back the covers and push her feet into ice cold slippers to make her way across the room to stoke the embers of a fire that served as both her heater and her light most of the time.

She'd found by keeping the heat only warm enough to keep the pipes from freezing that her propane would last a lot longer. Sure, it meant she practically lived in front of the fireplace in the once-cozy living room. But without money... She had to do what she had to do. Evie sighed. If only she could get herself to sculpt again.

A blast of wind blowing across the house brought a shower of snow swirling from the top of the porch. Evie shivered as it settled over her and she looked back at the man crumpled at the bottom of her steps. She gasped. Somehow in her musing, she'd almost forgotten about him.

"What am I supposed to do with him?" she asked, looking skyward and was rewarded with another flurry of snow. "Thanks!" she said as she turned and marched back up the steps and through the door that she slammed shut. She'd learned the hard way how easily the heat escaped through an open door.

Pushing aside the old blanket she'd hung over the entrance to the hallway that led to the rest of the house, she tried not to look around much as she went into the closet in her parents' first floor bedroom to retrieve a couple of thick quilts. Sadness gripped her when she glanced at their wedding photo hanging on the wall. A thin layer of dust had settled along the top and crevices of the frame and slightly obscured the image of the smiling couple. My, how they had loved one another.

She glanced at the bed that had been empty for almost six months now. The hand-crocheted coverlet still had the indentation where her dad had sat to put on his shoes for the last time before leaving the house. Evie lowered her eyes and walked out of the room, making sure to close the door against the cold. It was too bad she couldn't block the coldness from her heart as easily.

Going through the living room, Evie tossed one of the quilts toward the sofa. She missed but didn't bother to stop and pick it up. Instead, she went to the door, paused for a moment to pray she'd imagined the stranger, and yanked open the door to see she had not. There he lay looking as if he hadn't moved a muscle since she'd left him.

As she stood at the bottom of the steps, she looked heavenward again and clenched her teeth. Why was the universe using her as its outhouse?

She shook her head. It was too late to worry about that now. She needed to get this man moved inside or risk watching him freeze to death on her stoop. There was no way she could move the stranger on her own. She wouldn't have the necessary strength, except in her angel form.

Closing her eyes, she put her palms together and turned in a slow circle while softly mumbling the words she needed to summon her wings and transform.

Chapter 3

Adam watched the little angel pace back and forth along the same path she'd been treading for... he had no idea how long, only that he'd been watching her for the past twenty minutes or better. Ever since he'd awakened he'd kept his eyes mostly closed, taking in what little he could see to get a feel for his surroundings, while trying to remember what had happened. He vaguely recalled his truck going into a ditch, walking through a lot of snow, and falling... and a dog.

"What happened to the dog?" he mumbled, slowly craning his neck to look at the woman.

Freezing in her tracks, her dark brows flying up toward her hairline, she stared back. She didn't move as he moved into a sitting position in his spot on the floor beside the fireplace, though she looked as if she might bolt at any second. She needn't worry, he thought. Groaning, he reached up to feel the lump on the back of his head.

"You... took a... na... nasty fall and h... hit your head pretty hard," she stammered through the sentence.

Adam nodded, his vision swimming a bit with the motion. With a deep breath, he pushed himself up, swaying unsteadily on his feet. He reached his hand to feel his back. His clothes were surprisingly dry... not completely, but more so than he'd expected, leaving him to believe he must have been out for quite a while. He really needed to get ahold of someone to help get the truck unstuck.

"Do you think…" he began, only to let his words trail off when he realized she'd moved closer to the front door… or what he assumed was the door he'd knocked on earlier. He also noticed for the first time that she had the fireplace poker in hand.

"Hey." He spoke in a soothing voice perfected over the many years of being a guardian angel. "Don't worry. I'm not going to hurt you. From one angel to another, surely you can sense that."

She'd been rocking ever so slightly from foot to foot, but she stopped at his words. Head cocked, she asked, "What do you mean?"

Adam chuckled. "I'm Adam, a guardian angel. And you are…?"

She didn't answer at first, just continued to stare. When she found her voice, she asked him what made him think she was an angel.

Adam shrugged. "Just a hunch," he crossed his fingers behind his back as he told the white lie. "And… I might have come to just long enough to see you change when we were outside." He'd never been good at lying. It just wasn't his nature, though when the little angel began to shuffle again, he kind of wished he had kept to his original statement.

"If you're really an angel, show me your wings." Her demand was punctuated with an air of someone asking with a please at the end instead of a hard command.

With a sigh, Adam slowly shook his head and put his hands, palms up, in front of him. "I wish I could, but it doesn't work that way for us. It's a bit different for guardian angels. I can't just summon them, but I can assure you it's not in our nature to hurt people."

Shoulders squaring, chin coming up, the angel whose name he still didn't know stopped her nervous shuffling and stared at him until he felt downright uncomfortable.

"Well, I'm not looking for a guardian angel. I don't need your help. I don't want it, so you can just take yourself right on out the door and back where you came from."

Stunned by her words, Adam was silent for a few seconds before he shrugged again. "I… I don't know what to say. I… really don't think I'm here to help you. Quite the contrary, it seems." He touched the back of his head which was already starting to feel better, thanks to the increased speed at which guardian angels healed. He'd keep that to himself for now though, because, unless he was being delusional, he thought he might just be starting to feel that slight tingle of apprehension he had at the beginning of every new case, which meant he'd need to find a reason to stay there for a while. "Besides that, my truck's in a ditch and it's starting to get dark. I doubt anyone's looking for me and I'm guessing I'll get little help at this hour…"

"Well, you can't stay here. Don't you have a phone or radio? Surely you thought to call for help."

Her shoulders sunk as Adam shook his head before reaching into his pocket. He pulled out his cellphone and looked at it. He'd had no signal at Mr. Vincent's and, as he'd suspected, he still had none.

"They don't use radios in the trucks because we all have cell phones, only…" He held up his phone. "No bars.

No signal." After a brief pause, he looked around but didn't see what he was looking for. "Maybe I could use your landline?"

The angel was already shaking her head before he finished.

Adams brows raised, especially when her hand went to the doorknob. Was she really going to kick him out? Just like that?

"Uhm. Maybe you can tell me how far I am from town then? Or maybe even the next house, considering…" He motioned toward the darkening window. "Perhaps you'd feel more comfortable if you'd turn on some lights…"

The little angel slumped back against the door, her head dropping forward, shoulders down in defeat.

"I can't believe this," she whispered.

Adam didn't say or do anything. He could see that she was working through her thoughts and alternatives.

With a huffing sigh, she lifted her head and looked him squarely in the eyes. "Look, Mister. I don't know who you are or why you're here. Hopefully, you're telling the truth and you just put your truck in a ditch. I'm guessing from what you've said that you were on a business call, so with any luck your boss will think to send someone to find you once he realizes you're missing. Until then… just sit down and keep your distance." She motioned to the big recliner near the fire where he stood.

Adam nodded, fighting the urge to salute her. Instead, he walked over to the chair and sank into it. He had a feeling this woman's sense of humor had taken a hiatus and she would not have appreciated his silly gesture. He definitely felt no humor from her in his empathetic core… only mistrust and pain that left him wondering who had hurt her so deeply, and why. Immediately, his guardian heart wanted to protect her. He settled for trying to find something that might lighten the mood.

Laughing a little, he looked toward the window. "I know it's staying light a little longer every day, but it sure feels like it gets dark awfully early."

She followed his gaze, her head snapping back to look at him after a brief second. She nodded. "Especially with all this snow. Where exactly did you say you went off the road?"

Adam scratched the top of his head, wishing he knew the area better. "I'm not quite certain. I was on my way back from a job for a gentleman by the name of Vincent. Do you know him? Older man. Widowed, I think from the way he talked."

"Everyone pretty much knows everyone around here. It's a decent sized island. It lets a body spread out but not get lost… usually."

Adam noticed a deepening of the sadness in her eyes as she said the words. Who was she hiding from? Or what? Maybe it wasn't a person at all. All he really knew was that the pain in her heart was palpable. She was hurting and she was hiding. He jumped when she began speaking again.

"I know him. He's bout twelve, maybe fifteen miles or so up the main road."

She nodded when his brows went up and he thought a smile almost made it to her mouth… a mouth framed by the sweetest lips he ever remembered seeing.

"I, uh. I guess it's a good thing I didn't try to walk back that way... speaking of walking... I suppose the dog that led me here belongs to you?" He was surprised when she shook her head. "That's so odd. He seemed to know exactly where he was headed."

The angel shrugged. "He probably lives on one of the other farms. Though Vincent's farm is the closest. I would have thought you'd have seen it there. What did he look like?" she asked.

Adam scrubbed his fingers over his cheeks and chin, feeling the prickly growth from where he hadn't shaved for the past couple of days. He'd let his beard grow over the holidays only to shave it after the New Year. He'd been assured the snow was a fluke, that it wouldn't stick around. Last week he'd decided he needed his beard back if the crazy weather was going to continue. Now, he was sure glad he'd started it. Anything was better than nothing against the freezing cold.

"I suppose he could have come from the St. George farm. You have to take a completely different road out of town to get there, but our fields do butt up against one another. It would be a hard trek in all this snow..." Evie raised a brow and cocked her head as she came closer and sank down on the end of the sofa as far away from him as possible. "What did you say he looked like?"

Adam bit off a chuckle when she tactfully re-asked the question he'd left unanswered when he'd gone on his tangent of thinking about beards and snow. He repeated the motion of rubbing his stubble before commenting. "Big. He had to be the biggest dog I've ever seen. Not fat, though.

More… tall. With lots and lots of shaggy white fur. Only, it was clean, and it didn't look tangled at all."

He hadn't thought of that until he was trying to remember the dog. Every other long-haired dog he'd ever come across had been pretty scraggly looking. Except for the show dogs owned by that one lady he'd had to save in Philadelphia several years earlier. Now, her dogs were immaculate. Always. Not a hair out of place, even when they were playing. Just like their owner. Thankfully, Adam had been able to help her see that she didn't need herself or everything else in her life to be so perfect in order to be happy.

Adam looked at the angel and wondered if he'd ever see her smile. The truth was, without the fire, he wasn't so sure he'd be able to see her at all! He glanced around wondering why she hadn't bothered to turn on the lights. He started to ask her then realization dawned. She hadn't been able to let him use her phone because she didn't have one. And the lights were off because there was no electricity to run them. He looked at the heavy blanket hung over an opening out of the living room and knew he was right. Whatever had torn up her heart had also robbed her of her livelihood. Geez. If anyone needed his help, it was most definitely her.

"So, do you think anyone will be coming this direction tonight that will find my truck?" he asked her.

She shook her head. "Not unless they're actively looking," she told him.

"I wonder if they'd even be able to see it. A white truck half buried in snow." He could see her stiffening up at his statement. "Look, I know you don't want me here, but... I really don't know what choice I have... unless you want to drive me into town?" He wondered why they hadn't thought of that earlier, though she was already shaking her head before the last word was out of his mouth.

"I don't drive anymore. Besides, none of the cars... I doubt any of them would start. It's been a good six months..." She looked away, blinking furiously.

Adam watched as she rubbed a finger beneath one eye and cleared her throat before looking back at him.

"All I have is the four-wheeler. If you want to use it, you're welcome to do so. It might not be a bad idea to tag your truck. I'm sure we have a red cloth around here you could use. My mom..." She was quiet again for a few seconds before continuing. "She was a quilter. She had baskets of scraps in every color."

Adam smiled. "I'm glad she did." He pointed to the pile of quilts in front of the fireplace. "I'm assuming she made those."

The angel nodded and sighed before leaning farther back into the sofa cushions.

"You're right. It probably would be good to tag the truck. My boss won't think about me not returning tonight, but he will when he gets to the shop tomorrow morning and his truck is gone. I'm sure he'll either send someone or head this way himself when he can't reach me."

Adam pulled his phone out of his pocket and looked at it again. Still no bars and it was almost out of power. He pressed the button to turn it off. With no electricity, there was no way to charge it so he may as well conserve what little energy it had left.

Yes, tagging the truck was a good idea. There was only one problem with that plan... he had no idea how to get from the end of her driveway back to the main road. Without the dog leading the way he could very well find himself in another drift over his head. He told the angel as much and she laughed. Only it was a sad, resigned sound that made him want to go to her as she got to her feet. He resisted, knowing he still needed to keep his distance if he was ever going to win her trust.

"I'll have to show you the way. Only you're going to need something thicker than what you have on. The temperatures will have dropped even farther now that the sun has gone down," she told him as she went toward the thick blanket-turned-door on the far side of the room. "You're fortunate your truck went off on the side that it did. Had you gone the other direction, you might have found yourself on the lake... or in it. As cold as it's been, I'm still not sure the ice is thick enough to support a vehicle."

The thought made Adam shiver. It was beginning to sound more and more like he was the one who needed a guardian angel. Perhaps he did have one and he just didn't know. He'd done that a time or two... played invisible guardian, though always to mere mortals. He'd never heard of a guardian who had a guardian.

Chapter 4

Adam was still pondering the possibility when she returned, her arms laden with outer wear.

"These belonged to my sister's husband. He was a little shorter than you and a bit rounder, but I'm thinking they won't be too bad."

She handed him a pair of thick, bibbed pants... the kind a hunter might wear. While he pulled them on over his jeans, she laid a pair of wool socks, and a Sherpa lined Cryder jacket on the couch. Beneath them, she had a matching pile of clothing for herself, plus facemasks and gloves.

"They lived up north until just after Lilia was born. When Trevor was killed, my sister brought her back here..."

Although he was dying to know all the gritty details, Adam kept himself from asking. She had already opened up more to him since she'd resigned herself that she couldn't just give him the boot and close her eyes only to open them to find him gone and her life back to normal. He had sensed the decision had been a huge struggle for her. That was one of the perks of being a guardian angel. He may not be able to read minds, but his senses were sharper than humanly possible, and his intuition was at a prime.

He didn't look at her again until he'd finished pulling

on his outerwear. That's when he realized she'd changed out of her loungers and into real clothes. She might have actually combed her hair as well, though it was hard to tell since she'd pulled it into a low ponytail at the back of her head. The high neck of her sweater and her hair away from her face really accentuated her beauty. Even without makeup, she was breathtaking. It wasn't until she thinned her lips that Adam realized he'd been staring. He smiled and turned away, attempting to focus his attention elsewhere while she finished.

Taking a couple of steps toward one of the rough-hewn shelves that lined the large, rock fireplace, Adam reached for a photograph. He turned it so that the light of the fire better illuminated the faces.

"Is this your family?" he asked when he sensed the angel had moved to his side.

He looked at her and she nodded before taking the picture from him, though she didn't put it back right away. Instead, she ran her fingers across the glass that covered the faces, stopping only briefly over each one until she came to a little girl standing beside where she sat on the bottom step of the big farmhouse.

She took a deep breath and let it out slowly before she spoke. "That was taken... not last summer but the one before that," she told him. Adam nodded and she continued "Those are my parents, Caleb and Ramona McCormick. And my sister, Caroline." She pointed to each before her finger, again, rested on the little girl.

Adam watched as she opened her mouth to speak, but only sighed and shook her head before moving past him to put the photograph back on the shelf.

"We'd better get going," she whispered before clearing her throat and continuing more boldly. "We'll need what little we have left to keep us on the road and out of the lake. I'm surprised the Greely's haven't had it plowed."

Adam chuckled. He recognized the name as one of the customers who had put their solar panel installation on hold because they were heading to a warmer climate until the snow melted. He shared his insight with the angel when she lifted a brow in question to his chuckle.

The angel nodded. "I suppose that's the smartest thing to do. Most of these farmers are probably beside themselves since they're used to putting in their crops toward the end of February. If it keeps this up much longer, even if it all melts by then, it's going to be too wet to plant. I'm sure they feel like they're already behind on preparing their fields."

Not knowing a thing about farming but wanting to continue the conversation, Adam asked if that's the way she felt about her farm.

The angel snorted. "This farm was my dad's baby, not mine. I can't run it, so I don't know what's going to become of it."

She froze and he sensed she was unsure why she'd told him that. She looked around the room as if seeing it anew then shrugged.

"I suppose I'll have to sell it at some point."

Adam could hear the sadness in her voice and he scrambled for a solution, anything to help ease her pain. "Maybe you could hire someone to work the fields... or even lease them to one of the other farmers. You said there was another farm whose fields butted up to yours, didn't you?"

She nodded and her brows furrowed. He could practically see her thinking, her mind probing the possibilities.

"I'd never thought of that," she told him as she motioned for him to put on his facemask, hat, and gloves. She grabbed a small lantern from a shelf near the door, struck a match and lit it while he finished.

The wind hit him hard the second he stepped out the door behind her. Adam sucked in when the cold air met his face and traveled down to sting his lungs. He was glad when she headed toward the smaller barn nearby, though the relief would be short-lived. Inside was a mowing tractor, a vehicle covered with a dusty mat, a truck that looked as if it had seen better days, and two four-wheel ATVs—one camo, the other red. Without a word, the angel handed him the lantern and set about unhooking a wagon from one ATV, only to sling a large, hard-plastic crate onto the back rack. She looked around for a minute then grabbed a rope, a couple of giant flashlights that almost blinded Adam when she tested them, and two wool-looking blankets.

When she jumped on one and motioned for Adam to get on the other, he hesitated.

"How do you know they'll run?" he asked.

Although he couldn't see her mouth for the scarf she'd tied around the lower part of her face, he felt certain she had thinned her lips at the stupidity of his question. It had seemed logical to him. If none of the vehicles would run, how did she know these recreational vehicles would?

"I've been using that one to gather firewood." She pointed to the one he was to ride, the one whose wagon she'd removed. "And this one to check the mail. I've been syphoning off the gas from the vehicles ever since I realized none of them would turn over anymore."

Adam nodded. "It's probably just the batteries. I'm sure a mechanic could have them running in no time."

Evie's only answer was to turn the key and rev the engine of the red four-wheeler. Adam set the lantern down and moved forward to open the double doors a bit wider before he hustled back to the camo-colored ATV and jumped on. When he paused just outside the door, preparing to shut the barn, she motioned to him and shook her head.

Okay then, Adam thought. If she wasn't concerned, then neither was he. Instead, he pulled his scarf up to cover as much of his face as possible, revved his engine, and raced off after her, not wanting to lose sight of the taillights that were his beacon in the ever-darkening night. He looked up and said a little prayer that maybe, just this time, the moon would be bright enough that the reflection off the snow would help light their way to and from his truck. They might get there before the night fully engulfed them, but there was no way they could go to and from without a little help.

At the end of the tree-lined drive, she paused and waited for him to pull up beside him.

"Be sure you stay right behind me from here on. Don't stray from one side to another. I, uh… I'm going by feel." Her nervous laughter rang above the machines. "I've been down this road at least a million times. Piece of cake, right?!"

He saw her shoulders rise and fall in what he could only imagine was a huge sigh, then watched as she gunned the engine of her machine and took off.

"Piece of cake," he repeated, doing the only thing he could. He followed her.

Chapter 5

As they ate up the snow, Adam's heartbeat revved in rhythm with his machine and he was sure that if he were a normal human, his blood pressure would have been high enough to have sent him to a hospital. Not only was the little angel going at breakneck speed, but there was an eerily odd glow in the distance. It appeared they were headed straight toward it.

The closer they got, the brighter it got, and he began to wonder if maybe his truck was on fire. He'd turned it off, hadn't he? Yes, he could remember that. He'd turned it off, pushed his way out, and even shut and locked the door. The lights were automatic so they should have turned off as well.

As if a switch flipped on in his brain, Adam realized what was happening. He laughed at himself for not thinking about it sooner. It wasn't his truck, but what was *in* his truck that was making the lights. Part of his day had been taking down Christmas decorations… solar powered strands of lights. Piled on top of Mr. Vincent's too small panels were enough twinkie lights to… well, to make his truck bed look as if someone had built an electric bonfire in there. Adam hadn't noticed the lights earlier because their little solar panel control boxes stored up their power throughout the day and turned the lights on at dusk. He hadn't thought to manually shut them off when he was taking them down, so there they were, illuminating his truck and creating the perfect beacon for them to follow.

The angel stopped just short of the main road and turned back to look at him. She motioned and he carefully maneuvered his machine into position beside her.

"I don't think anyone would have missed your truck if they'd wandered by," she yelled across the sound of the engines.

Adam nodded. "I forgot about the Christmas lights," he confessed.

For the first time, he thought he might have seen the corners of her eyes crinkle with the hint of a smile. Adam felt a strange flutter just below his ribcage. It was as unfamiliar to him as it had been for her beauty to have taken away his breath. What was it about this mystical angel that caused his senses to scramble?

"I'm guessing they'll turn themselves off come morning, right?" she asked.

Adam nodded then audibly voiced a "yes" since she wasn't looking at him to see his head move.

"Then it's still a good thing we came."

Without another word, she eased her machine to the edge of the main road, looked both ways and drove across, parking just shy of what had to be the edge of the pavement. She had pulled off her gloves and was rummaging in her pockets when Adam stopped beside her. Cautiously, he got off his machine and took the red cloth she'd retrieved from the depths of her coat. She followed his lead, swinging her leg over and standing up, stopping at the crate on his machine to retrieve a stick he hadn't seen her put in. He smiled. She'd thought of everything.

When he stepped off the pavement and into the drift, Adam was sure glad he still had on his heavy work boots, but he was even happier she'd thought to have them don the thick pants and jackets. Without them, the cold of the snow would have surely seeped in and settled around their bones. The thought made Adam shiver.

"Are you cold?" she asked.

He could see her assessing whether he was telling the truth when he shook his head.

Adam laughed. "Thankfully, no. I was just thinking about how cold it would be if you hadn't properly outfitted us."

Again, he thought he saw the corners of her eyes crinkle, though she didn't say anything. Adam didn't either. Instead, he held out his hand as she began to follow him into the drift. As she reached for it, she slipped a little and ended up colliding into him. Instinctively, Adam wrapped his arms around her, pulling her to him to keep her upright.

Staring down into her sky-blue eyes, Adam could have sworn the world stopped if only for a split second. Never in his life, and he'd lived a good while, had he ever had such an overwhelming desire to let his lips settle over someone else's. He felt... *something*. He wasn't quite sure just what that something was, but if he had to guess, her expression said that she felt it too.

"Oh my," she whispered, ducking her head just as he began to move his face toward hers. "We... we'd better get done here and head back. It's, uh, starting to get dark really fast." She pulled away from him and turned toward his truck, making her way through the snow that was well above her waist.

Adam stood rooted to the same spot like an idiot. It wasn't until she almost slipped again that he shook himself out of it. Now was not the time to try to figure out what had happened.

The one thing he knew was that he needed to be careful to keep his feelings in check. After all, the number one rule for guardian angels was that they could never get involved with their charges—the ones they were sent to help or protect. To do so meant they had to give up their wings.

Not literally give them up, of course. It wasn't like their wings would be ripped from them, but it did mean their days of being a guardian angel and the privileges that came with that would be over. Adam couldn't imagine that. Or he thought he couldn't. He put his hand over his stomach. Even covered with layers and layers of thick clothing, he could still feel the quiver inside as he looked at the little angel whose name he still didn't know.

"Stop it," he whispered to himself as he shook it off and stepped forward to help her secure the stick with the red flag so that someone would, hopefully see it.

"Put this in the window so they'll know where to find you." She brushed off his help and handed him a piece of paper from her pocket.

Carefully unfolding it, he saw there was an address written on it. He was impressed that she'd thought of that. He certainly hadn't.

"There are a lot of things you learn to do when you live out in the country," she told him.

Adam nodded. He was beginning to think she had a knack for fine details. He appreciated that. Normally he did as well, though they seemed to be taking turns taking the lead. That was another strange feeling, though it didn't feel all together bad. It seemed more like they were a team.

"Get that done so we can go," she told him, pointing to the paper she'd handed him.

Adam looked at the paper and realized he'd been standing there doing nothing. Not good, he told himself before he did as she'd said.

A few seconds later, they climbed out of the snow drift and back onto the ATVs.

"It's going to be harder going back," she called over the engines. "The clouds don't seem to be cooperating. Let's hope it doesn't start snowing again, at least before we hit the tree line."

Adam turned his face toward the sky and sighed. He wasn't used to having his prayers ignored, but the increasing clouds sure made it seem like his request for ample moonlight would go unheeded.

"Just take your time and be careful," he yelled.

The angel gave him a thumbs up and throttled her machine into action. Adam started to follow, then stopped. His heart slamming, he jumped off the ATV and slid back down the snowbank. Reaching his truck, he fished around in the bed and grabbed a bunch of the light strands. There was no reason they couldn't use them back at her place. They should still have several hours of light left and using them would be a lot better than just the fireplace. Maybe not quite as romantic. Not that he had any business with romantic notions.

Knowing he didn't have time to think about all of that, he rushed back to his ATV and threw the lights into the crate on the back. It made him laugh just a bit as he imagined how he'd look with his backside lit up. The ones he'd grabbed weren't blinking, otherwise he might have looked like a lightning bug.

Revving the engine, he raced toward the lights of the other machine, careful to make sure he stayed in her tracks.

Toward the end of the road, he caught up with her. Thankfully, she had slowed down a bit. He knew she was looking for the path.

"Feel your way," he whispered, and, for a few seconds, he thought she had done just that. She pointed to the outline of a tree up ahead and throttled up her machine again as she raced toward it, taking a left turn on the other side.

Adam watched in horror as her machine went airborne, flying through the night sky before landing with a thud as she sank into the snow. He slammed on his brakes and turned off his machine, pulling his facemask off so he could listen.

"Adam."

He heard his name over the muffled rumbling of the other ATV engine just before a thundering crack filled the night.

"No!" he screamed. No, this couldn't be happening. He knew in that instance that he'd waited his whole life for this woman. He couldn't lose her. Not this way. Not now.

He wasn't sure when he'd gotten off the camo-colored ATV. He couldn't remember tying one of the ropes to the vehicle and securing the other end to his waist. And he sure didn't recall grabbing several strands of Christmas lights, though when he got to the place where the ice had broken, he scattered them around the hole. He prayed, if nothing else, that maybe she'd be able to see the lights and that would help her know which way to swim.

"Come on," he whispered as he hooked one of the light strands to the other rope and fed them into the hole. He jiggled it around a bit, praying she'd see it.

Time seemed to drag for an eternity, though he knew only seconds had passed. He'd give her a few more before he did the only thing he knew to do. If she didn't surface, he'd have to go in after her. "Come on," he said again, his voice louder as he sat back on his haunches and started to unzip his coat.

Just as he began to pull his arms from the sleeves, he noticed bubbles on the water's surface. He held his breath and leaned forward, waiting. When a hand broke the surface, he grabbed it with an iron grip. The ice cracked a bit more as he hauled her weighty form out of the water, but there was no way he was letting go. Thankfully, the surface held and he carefully inched backwards until he hit the bank of the lake where he stood and pulled them both up to safety.

After a few steps, Adam dropped to his knees. He cradled her limp body against his as he sucked air. "You have to be okay," he croaked out. His chin dropped down, his forehead against her nose as the tears began to drop from his cheeks to hers. He'd already decided that he'd trade his life as a guardian angel in a heartbeat if it meant she would survive... if it meant there was a chance for them. "You have to be okay," he said again as he rocked them back and forth. "I... I don't even know what to call you."

"Evie."

The word was spoken so soft Adam thought he had imagined it.

"Evangeline," she said on a cough. "But I've always been called Evie." She coughed again and Adam sat up and leaned her forward, patting her back as gently as he would that of a baby.

"Evie," he whispered, then said again a bit louder.

Adam and Evie. Now if that didn't show that the Big Guy had a sense of humor, he didn't know what did.

He smiled, the cold causing his cheeks to sting. He really shouldn't have pulled off his face mask earlier, though he knew he was anywhere near as uncomfortable as Evie. She had begun to shake. He needed to get her back to the farmhouse where she could get warmed up.

Struggling to his feet, he lumbered over to the remaining ATV and sat her on it while he grabbed the blankets she'd put in the crate. He worked quickly to get her wrapped up, otherwise the wind against her wet clothes as they drove would drop her body temperature to an even more dangerous level. If he didn't think he'd freeze, he'd give her his jacket as well, though caution told him he needed it if he was to remain well and alert. The reality was, he had to do everything he could to keep his senses because she was going to need him.

He climbed onto the machine and wrapped his arms

around her to where he could reach the handlebars. By then, her body was shaking so intensely that he had to grip the controls with iron fists. That wasn't easy to do with freezing cold hands, though he welcomed it. As long as she was shaking, that meant her body was working to keep her alive.

Adam closed his eyes. He bowed his head and prayed harder than he'd ever prayed in his life, asking if, for this one last act as a guardian angel, he could just get them back safely to the farmhouse so that he could get her warmed up.

He opened his eyes and watched as the clouds parted and the moon lit up trees a short distance away. They were the trees that lined her driveway.

Chapter 6

Adam left Evie in front of the blazing fireplace. She was still shaking so much he wasn't sure if she could remove her wet clothing herself, but he also sensed her apprehension with having him help. Had she been unconscious, he wouldn't have hesitated stripping them both down so he could use his own body heat to help raise hers. Not that he had a lot of extra heat at that moment, except... well, in areas he'd never really had to worry about before. He chuckled as he walked into the bathroom, wondering if this was what non guardians had to deal with.

"All in good time," he whispered to himself while he removed his wet clothing and replaced them with new attire that he'd found in the room Evie had directed him to. He pushed the soggy pile to the side and picked up the clothing he'd collected for her. Knowing Evie needed to warm up, he'd chosen the thickest loungewear he could find. He knew she wasn't in the clear yet, but the fact that she wanted to help herself and had the strength to try were good signs. In his heart, he felt a small flutter. He hoped it was a sign that everything would be okay.

Yes, Adam Springer was one hopeful ex-guardian angel as he walked back into the farmhouse living room and laid the clothing on the rug beside where Evie sat wrapped in the same quilts he'd been in earlier. He told her he was going to go make them something warm to drink while she got dressed and she pointed him toward the kitchen. He looked around as he went. He kind of liked this old farmhouse. It had a lot of character... and it had Evie. The first thing he'd do, if she'd allow it, would be to reinstate the electricity. Then, maybe his boss would sell him some solar panels at a discount... maybe the ones he'd removed from Mr. Vincent's house. He wouldn't need to pay for installation, since he already knew how to do that.

Adam chuckled. Maybe being a solar panel installer wasn't such a bad job after all. He wondered how it would compare to working a farm. There was a lot of manual labor involved in both...

Suddenly, as Adam stood in the outdated farmhouse kitchen, he could see his life before him... or at least a life he'd like to try to live.

Chapter 7

Evie watched Adam reenter the room from her spot in front of the fire. Her mouth watered a bit as she stared at the two steaming mugs he carried. Even in her thick pajamas and two heavy quilts, she was still so cold. If it hadn't been for the faint flicker of fire that had begun to build low in her abdomen, she might have thought she'd never be warm again, though she knew that was a different kind of warmth. Was she crazy to allow this man to stir these kinds of feelings in her? He was a stranger, after all.

He saved your life, her inner voice reminded her.

Yes, he had. In more ways than one.

"I still can't believe I misjudged where the driveway was," she told him as she took the mug he offered. "I could have sworn there were other trees where I turned."

Adam settled on the floor next to her, though leaving a respectable distance.

Evie smiled a little as she ducked her head. He seemed to have some old-fashioned values. She liked that.

"It was so dark out, I'm surprised we made it as far as we did, really," he said after a few seconds of silence.

Evie sensed he was staring at her and she looked up into deep, pensive eyes—eyes that investigated one's very soul. Eyes that belonged to a guardian angel. *Her* guardian angel. She was so thankful he'd been there for her.

A single tear dropped onto her cheek. He moved closer

and reached to wipe it away, his finger warm against her cool cheek.

"Why didn't they have a guardian angel?" she whispered.

"They?" Adam frowned, his brows drawing down in momentary confusion before he looked over his shoulder at the photograph he'd picked up earlier. "Your family?" He nodded when she did. "I'm sorry. Wh... what happened? Can you tell me?"

At first, Evie shook her head but then she nodded even though several minutes would pass before she found her voice. She leaned against him and told him of the awful car wreck that had taken the lives of the four people she loved the most.

"Why?" she cried, her tears soaking his shirt right above his heart.

He held her, stroking her hair and whispering soothing sounds. "I don't know, sweetheart. I truly wish I did. There are just some things that seem to have no reason, when really, it's all just a part of a bigger picture that none of us can see."

Evie contemplated that for a minute before she pulled back and looked at him. "Do you think they're okay? I mean... I know you don't know them, but... they really were good people. And little Lilia... she was so young."

Adam nodded and touched her nose with his own. "I'm certain they're okay," he told her. "If they were anything like you, and I have no reason to doubt they weren't, I can only imagine their next life has been glorious."

Evie sniffled as a few more tears ran down her cheeks.

How could she have forgotten the words her sister had spoken to her right before she passed from this life to the next? Caroline had told her she had glimpsed Heaven and it was the most beautiful place she'd ever seen. Her sister had smiled as she closed her eyes and squeezed Evie's hand for the last time.

"Tell my Lilia," she'd whispered when she'd leaned in to kiss Caroline's cheek. "Tell her who I am."

Evie slowly shook her head. "I didn't tell her soon enough," she said to Adam. His brows furrowed and she continued knowing the bombshell she was about to drop might well be enough to sever that strand of a relationship she thought had been starting to form between them. Still, she needed to tell him. She wanted no secrets between them.

"No one knew except my sister and her husband, but Lilia... she wasn't my niece. She was my daughter."

Evie waited for him to stiffen or pull away, but Adam only nodded, and she went on. "I was young, only sixteen, and I thought my high school boyfriend was the one I would spend the rest of my life with. It seemed logical when he pushed to take our relationship to the next level. After all, wasn't that what people who loved one another did?" A few more tears fell and Adam pulled her back against his chest. "After I found out and her father left, I didn't want to give her up. My sister and her husband offered to raise her until she was old enough for us to explain... only, she died. We never got to tell her. She never knew. Oh, Adam. It was my fault that they were taken away from me. I'm being punished..." she sobbed.

Adam shook his head and she grabbed the front of her

shirt, knotting it in her fist as she continued. "Sometimes it hurts so much I don't think there's any way I can go on without them."

"No, honey." He kissed the top of her head. "If you hadn't loved them so much it wouldn't be so hard. Things like this happen in life. It's not anyone's fault. It's not a punishment, even though it may feel like one. Just think how fortunate you are to have had someone in your life that you cared about so much that losing them hurts like it does. Not everyone has that... and you had four very dear people."

Evie sat back and stared at him. She'd never thought about it like that before. "I just wish I could see her one more time, to tell her who I am and that I love her so much."

He smiled at her. "You never know. Life is full of surprises. I mean... look at us. Less than half a day ago, we didn't even know one another and now, here we are.

Evie nodded. She wondered where they were headed. It felt to her as though they were embarking on a new beginning—something new for both of them.

Chapter 8

A few weeks later, Evie stood on the front porch of the old farmhouse and watched the thin plume of dust that gathered as Adam drove his work truck up the gravel drive. The snow had lasted only a short time after that crazy January night that could have well been the last for either of them.

The sound of the wind caressing the treetops caused her to look up. She pulled in a deep breath, enjoying the feel of the distant whispers of Spring that swirled around her.

She waited eagerly by the railing while her husband finished up inside the truck and got out before he raced up the steps to her.

"I missed you," he told her, the corners of his mouth lifting before he lowered his mouth to hers for a kiss filled with enough promise to last a lifetime.

He pulled back slightly and sniffed. "Something smells delicious... besides you," he teased, rubbing his nose against her cheek.

Evie laughed and pushed him away only to grab his hand before they slipped through the front door. "It's your favorite—pot roast with all the trimmings. I put two of them on right after you left this morning and let them slow cook through the day."

"Sounds heavenly. Good thing you cooked two since I'm starving."

Adam winked and Evie rolled her eyes. She knew that he knew she'd already sent one home with William, their new hired hand. He was young, but he seemed to know his way around the fields. He also seemed to appreciate the home-cooked meals Evie sent with him every Friday night and occasionally during the week, though she was thinking he may not be needing them much longer. She'd seen him talking to Mr. Vincent's granddaughter, Sarah, a few times in town and again at the Spring Extravaganza held at the big castle on the other end of the island last week. She figured he'd be with them just long enough for Adam to finish learning all he needed to know to take over the fields. He and Art Guthrie would have most of the houses on the island outfitted with solar panels by the end of summer. Then it would be more of a maintenance operation. They'd already discussed Adam's role in all of that, plus him helping with the Christmas decorating demands.

Evie thought of the lights that had been in Adam's truck that fateful night and how he'd thought seeing them was what had brought her to the surface after she'd crashed through the icy lake. If it had been them, she'd seen them as beautiful blue butterflies with a larger yellow butterfly leading the way. He'd called to her, commanding her to fight, to swim because she had too much to live for, too many left to help... and she had Adam.

Giving her husband one more tight squeeze, she darted off to get dinner on the table while he changed out of his work clothes. Before they parted, he handed her a sheet of paper that she unfolded as she walked. It had the names and addresses of more people who wanted her little sculptures. Five more, to be exact.

Five! It was going to be a busy weekend.

After dinner, they sat on the sofa staring into the blazing fire, not because they needed it for warmth, but because they enjoyed it. The time they spent there was a pleasant reminder of their beginning, as well as a place to unwind or simply enjoy being close to one another like they were at that moment with Adam nibbling Evie's ear.

"Did you hear that?" Eve asked as she pulled away from him and scooted toward the edge of the sofa.

Adam hadn't heard a thing. He'd been too enthralled with the feel of her silky soft hair against his cheek and the fresh spring scent that was distinctly Evie.

"There!" She stood, pulling lightly to get him to follow her.

With a groan, he hauled himself up. The sooner she realized she'd imagined the sound, the faster they could get back to the soft sofa and cozy fire. He felt the tingle of excitement just thinking about having Evie in his arms again and admitted to himself that there was no better feeling. Not even that of having helped all the people he had throughout his years on Earth. He'd like to think maybe part of the reason it felt so good was because he had been part of the solution to Evie's regaining happiness. He'd saved the best for last, and boy had it been a doozie.

They were almost to the door when Adam finally heard the dog. He froze before pushing past Evie, his eyes and mouth both opened wide. There, in the little flower bed that rimmed the porch was the white blob.

"Stop him!" Evie yelled, running down the steps,

waving her hands in the direction of the dog whose paws and teeth were making a mess of the jonquils that were just shy of blooming.

When Evie called his name, Adam snapped out of his shock and he jumped down beside his wife while telling the dog to cease his antics.

"Come on, boy. You gotta get out of there before she takes a broom to you." He knew she would, too. He'd seen her go after a squirrel or two who'd wreaked havoc in the same area while trying to bury some of the peanuts Adam had put out for them. He couldn't fault her for it. This particular bed of flowers was special to her. It was one she and Lilia had planted together the spring her daughter had turned three.

"Go on." He clapped his hands and the dog took off across the newly-paved parking pad. Adam followed for a few steps, happy to see his old friend, though he froze as the dog twirled, morphing into an ethereal woman. He gasped when she waved and began to laugh. Adam couldn't believe it. The dog wasn't a dog at all and there was no *good boy*. No wonder she never came when he called. What woman wants to be called *here boy*!

Faster than his thoughts could fire, she morphed again. This time into a beautiful blue butterfly, very nearly the same color as his eyes. As she flew, she was joined by more blue butterflies. They race toward a single yellow butterfly whose wings begin to expand until there was a burst of light in the sky and it opened to reveal Heaven. There, a little girl stood holding a woman's hand. They both waved and Adam began to wave back, his hand dropping to his side when he heard a sob behind him.

He turned and realized Evie had been the target of their salutation.

"My baby," she whispered through her tears.

Adam stared at her then turned back to look at the two. Could it truly be? Was it really Evie's sister and daughter?

"I love you, Mommy," the little girl called, blowing a kiss that Evie pretended to catch.

Evie's sister smiled. "You asked me to make sure she knew, and I did. Though she already knew by the time I got to her."

Evie looked at Adam. During one of their many conversations, he'd told her Lilia would know. He'd been right.

He went to her, putting his arm around her shoulder and kissing the top of her head. Without removing her hands from over her mouth, she leaned into him. Tears streaming down her cheeks.

"Don't cry, Mommy. I want you to be happy, too."

Evie wiped at her tears with the sleeve of her shirt and sniffled a few times. "I am, baby. I'm just... so surprised to see you. It made me sad because you're not with me anymore, but I'm happy, so happy to see you." Her tears renewed and the little girl giggled.

"Grownups on Earth are so funny," she told Evie's sister who nodded. "Silly Mommy. I'm always with you. Can't you feel me in your heart?"

Evie covered her heart with her hands and nodded. "You're right," she told her. "You've always been right here, and you always will be, no matter what."

"No matter what," Lilia repeated, her already radiant smile widening.

Both Lilia and Caroline glanced over their shoulders as if hearing something Adam and Evie couldn't. Caroline nodded and squeezed the little girl's hand.

"We have to go now," she told them. "Goodbye, Evie. We'll see you again... when it's time." She turned her gaze on Adam and told him to take good care of her sister. He covered his heart and nodded.

Lilia waved, then paused. "Oh! I forgot. I'm sorry I wished for so much snow on Grandma's Christmas poinsettia last year. I know it lasted a long time, but it sure was pretty... and it brought Adam to you. Goodbye, Mommy. I love you!"

Evie tried to smile, even as more tears streamed down her cheeks. "It was beautiful, and I love you too, my angel."

Lilia giggled again as they turned, and the sky slowly began to close.

"She called me angel," they heard her say to Evie's sister. The sweet child's laughter floated down around them as clouds rushed in to fully obscure the opening.

Seconds later, the clouds moved away and were replaced by a beautiful sunset that would become the talk of the island in the days and weeks to come.

Evie realized in that moment that loved ones never fully leave. When we need them the most, they show up. It may come across as a reminiscent scent wafting on a gentle breeze, or a certain color reflected from a summer sky. Perhaps the sound of one's name whispered on the wind or a gentle, calming touch to the shoulder.

She looked at the sky streaked with blue and yellow, and then at Adam. No, her time here was not done. She may not be a guardian angel, but she could still help people find the right path, just like Adam had done for so many. Including her. Without him, she knew she wouldn't be there. She'd have sat in that farmhouse wasting away, mourning for a past that couldn't be replaced. That was no way to live... it wasn't her destiny.

Adam and Evie.

She smiled and looked toward the heavens. Her daughter had been correct, the snow had brought Adam to her, and it had been no coincidence. Someone had known they needed one another. Someone with a sense of humor.

Author Note

Whispers of Spring began as a short story that was supposed to take a weekend to write. Then I started working on it and Adam and Evie let me know their story needed a few more thousand words to tell it right. They grabbed hold of my heart, and my keyboard, and brought more than a few tears as I wrote the ending. I hope you enjoy this foray into the lives of these particular characters in my *Wings & Whispers Love Stories* as much as I enjoyed writing them.

Be on the lookout for more books in this series as well as others. Signing up for my Between the Pages newsletter is the best way to stay informed. You'll receive news and special offers as well as a couple of free books for signing up. You'll find the sign-up form and information at:

LindaBoulangerBooks.com/newsletter-sign-up

Until the next story…
Thank you for being a part of my dream,
Linda

Works by Linda Boulanger

An up-to-date list of all of Linda's works may be found at:

LindaBoulangerBooks.com/book-links

About Linda Boulanger

Linda Boulanger is an award-winning author of fantasy and historical romance whose interest in the Medieval era often figures into her books, though you may also find time travel, dragons, angels, fairies, and other mystical beings mixed into her stories. Having grown up in the magical land of Alaska, her imagination was her refuge when winter days got too cold, or she needed to hide away from overly large mosquitos in the summer. It was during those days that the storyteller was born, though it would take many years, and several hat changes, before she realized the voices in her head were characters screaming for their stories to be written.

When not traipsing into imaginary lands or designing book covers, Linda can be found spending time with her family in NE Oklahoma's Green Country.

About Linda Boulanger

Other place to find Linda:

Website
LindaBoulangerBooks.com

Facebook Page
facebook.com/AuthorLindaBoulanger/

Facebook Group
facebook.com/groups/543640686756594

Newsletter Singup
lindaboulangerbooks.com/newsletter-sign-up.html

BookBub
bookbub.com/authors/linda-boulanger

Amazon Author Page
amazon.com/Linda-Boulanger/e/B002NPYDC6

Twitter
twitter.com/LBoulangerBooks

Instagram
instagram.com/lindaboulangerbooks/

TikTok
tiktok.com/@medievallb